BEYOND THE THRESHOLD

∞

Kathleen Staley

ISBN-13:
978-1542684224

∞

Ideas presented are solely intended for entertainment. Stories are fabricated and have no relation to actual persons or events.

Venice Beach Angel

On a sunny afternoon in Los Angeles, a homeless man with a long beard, sunhat, dressed in ragged clothing and no shoes called out to the passersby.

"Welcome to my humble abode. Sit with me awhile. Once you cross the threshold and enter the domain of altered reality you will never be the same."

As people walked by they made comments such as-

"Look at that old geezer. He must have popped the wrong pill or a whole bottle. Maybe he fell down the rabbit hole and joined Alice. He is so weird."

A local vendor said "Every day he sits in a lotus position at the foot of the Venice Beach Angel sculpture and talks to people about going "beyond the threshold." He says that the mosaic of mirrors in the sculpture focuses frequencies or something like that. I think he is a nutcase but some say that he is very wise and spiritually enlightened."

Another vendor added "I heard that he was one of the first doctors to try LSD and when he made his findings public, he was silenced by the government. He allegedly acquired knowledge of major conspiracy theories and in lectures began exposing frightening and insidious plots to manipulate and exterminate the masses."

"Oh, yeah, I heard about him too. He was a Professor of Astronomy and Physics. He supposedly went on an expedition to the Antarctic and soon after he got back, he went crazy before he could tell anyone what happened."

" Everyone thought we went insane after taking too much acid but I read somewhere that the professor claimed that he was abducted by aliens. He lost his job and all of his friends and family turned their backs on him."

"He was a real genius, like Nikola Tesla and taught classes about electromagnetic energy , time-travel and inter-dimensional physics."

"Look at him now, he is just a sad old man without a home. I feel sorry for him but I would bet that he has some amazing stories to tell."

"It is a shame that people took too much LSD and burned themselves out. Some ended up in mental institutes or on the streets."

With fifty dollars in his hand, a seventeen year old Nate Miller, carrying a large cup with soda pop, dressed in black approached the man that called himself Al.

Motioning with his hand, Al called out "Come, come into my domain, can I help you my brother? I am receiving messages clearly today and the frequencies tell me that you are troubled and curious about what is going beyond the threshold."

The boy with anarchy symbols on his shirt, pierced nose and ears and wearing black eye makeup announced "I want to try LSD. Do you sell it?"

Indignantly Al replied "NO absolutely not. I may be homeless and a bit destitute but I am not a drug dealer. My experiences with LSD were controlled experiments and opened my mind beyond what most people would be able to handle. I learned things that were so frightening that if I revealed the truth, I would be locked up or probably killed. My advice is to never use drugs, especially LSD."

Nate asked "What do you mean? What sort of things are you talking about? I won't tell."

Al replied "It doesn't matter if you tell or not. They are always watching. Shadow organizations control everything and the government people don't even know about what is really going on. They want to wipe out most of the people in the world and are actively involved in population control. Our food, the water we drink and the ideas we have are all being controlled by earthly, extraterrestrial and inter-dimensional entities. You have to be very careful about words and deeds or they will silence you."

With sarcasm Nate said "Sounds like paranoia to me, dude. My dad says there are no such things as extraterrestrials or conspiracies to kill off the population."

Looking squarely at Nate, Al remarked "Young man, you are naïve. Life is nothing like television, movies or news programs. Everything we see is by intent and is meant to control you, including the clothes you wear and the soft drinks consumed in quantity."

Gladly accepting the cash, Al said "This story will give you an idea of what I mean, without revealing anything specific. It is absolutely true but the names are different. It is best to think in terms of fiction and fantasy, otherwise it would be too unbelievable and could be dangerous."

Ring of Truth

Research student Fred Marino discovered the existence of an organized assault on the human race but no one believed him. After years of studies he showed his associate and roommate Bernard the vast collection of evidence, including pictures, videos and audio recordings. He was convinced that there was a worldwide conspiracy to keep the existence of an alien invasion a secret or at least a human generated assault by the food industry. The focus of his work involved proving his theories and gathering evidence to support his claims.

The research led to many other avenues of thought but everything he read seemed to fit together. Because of his kind soul, he wished to teach others about his findings but he remained private. A common theme in the research was health care and it led to places that appeared sinister in nature. Manufacturing of synthetic foods and processing of mass quantities of drugs also piqued his curiosity. He was determined to uncover corruption in the industry.

While sharing his ideas with Bernard, with a solemn tone Fred said "I believe a variety of earthly and extraterrestrial entities are watching and waiting for us to destroy each other so they can take over Earth."

Bernard rolled his eyes and clucked his tongue.

Fred continued "The majority of the population wants to achieve world peace but secret forces are working against us. It is curious and ironic that every time it seems we can overcome the violence, something happens to incite anger. I think our food is being poisoned intentionally, in order to control the population.

Bernard commented "You are paranoid and spend way too much time on the computer."

Smirking, Fred replied "Maybe I do spend a lot time researching but at least I am open minded, unlike you who wouldn't believe in aliens even if they came and knocked on your door. Think of all the junk food you eat- it is manufactured, genetically modified and poisonous. That at least should concern you. They are watching us and monitoring everything."

Bernard chuckled "Ha,ha, you are probably right but "they" are merely greedy humans. I don't believe in little green or gray men or any of that nonsense. If strangers knocked on my door and they were cordial to me, I might invite them in for tea. Almost everything on the Internet is either a hoax or the ramblings of individuals with too much time on their hands. I'm not sure about food but I eat what I like and I am in perfect health." He coughed and rubbed his forehead to ease his throbbing headache.

"You are burying your head in the sand, Bernard. I happen to know that a satellite dish in China detected a fleet of ships from another galaxy, headed to Earth. According to the reports, the aliens will attack and shut down Internet and all networks will be destroyed. Without the Internet we are powerless to get information. Only the elite with resources will control the masses and the elite will be controlled by the invaders. I think it has something to do with pyramids and their alignment to the Orion star-system. They might be landing bases for extraterrestrials, you never know."

Grumbling, Bernard replied "I think you are exaggerating and perhaps have seen too many sci-fi films. What about when there was no Internet? Humans lived without it for centuries and they figured out plenty of ways to wage war, destroy the environment and ruin the economy. The elite have always controlled the masses."

Fred continued "Yes that is true but they have never faced an enemy of this magnitude. According to my research, intergalactic visitors have been here for centuries. They arrived and remained to monitor and prevent nuclear war. I read that Nikola Tesla discovered their existence and learned about inter-dimensional travel. He was the first to harness the power needed to stop the invaders but he was silenced by the government and energy corporations."

With a serious expression Fred continued "The whole picture is frightening and I have only touched the surface. Maybe the reason for so many films with extraterrestrials is to prepare us for the truth of eminent invasion."

Bernard scoffed "Not everything is part some conspiracy. You are a lunatic but your ideas are entertaining. Let me know if you meet any aliens. We will all have tea and discuss the situation, ha, ha." He grabbed a handful of candy and devoured the sweets.

That night Fred felt restless. He sat at the computer desk and scrolled through endless information concerning secret societies, space research, reptilians and wondered about malevolent and benevolent forces. Gradually he put his head down to rest and fell asleep. With symbols, numbers, theories and images spinning in his head, he entered the dream world.

In a vivid dream he turned on the computer to search for job openings. With many skills he expected to find an assortment of opportunities to choose from. All of the queries diverted and directed him to a webpage entitled Ring of Truth, ROT.

Fred attempted to navigate away from the page but it would not let him exit or shut down. The only apparent way to clear the page was to open the file and read the information.

It prompted the user with a questionnaire and required personal information and resume. The company claimed to be hiring research assistants for a global peace project involving agriculture and manufacture of food for the masses. It seemed to be a noble cause and he continued.

A video showed a state-of-the-art facility with lodging, health care, self-contained structures for each worker in which all amenities were provided. From the outside the building resembled a stack of discs, each level rotated, inner-connected with elevator shafts and conveyor belts.

Although it appeared benevolent and provided a desirable income, Fred had the distinct impression that it was sterile, mechanical and perhaps a façade for a sinister organization. He imagined working amongst robotic employees and he laughed at the thought of having to serve alien, reptilian supervisors. His imagination ran wild and a series of bizarre scenarios played in his mind and left him overwhelmed with curiosity.

Later that afternoon Fred drove to ROT facility and was greeted cordially at the main gate. A tour-guide Stanley led to the various levels where the controlled environment made the visitors feel welcome.

With a blank expression Stanley announced "This is our pride and joy. Our facility has been built to withstand earthquakes, hurricanes and maintains weather control within the boundaries of the complex."

"When our employees are hired, they are treated with the utmost respect and we endeavor to fulfill all needs. Each worker will live in their own module and all amenities served. Once inside our hive you will not wish to leave. Happiness and fulfillment will be yours. We insert a special computer chip in to each worker for control and to assure loyalty"

For a brief moment Stanley's green-yellow eyes appeared more reptilian than human and his open mouth revealed sharp, pointed teeth. Fred felt a sense of foreboding and recalled the information concerning extraterrestrials, then decided to leave. He informed Stanley that he was not interested and wished to leave.

"Wait, are you sure you do not wish to learn more about our program?"

"No thank-you, Sir, but I would like to leave now. Please unlock the door and allow me to go."

"Very well young man, you may leave but this is a chance of a lifetime. If you stop now, you will regret it."

"I'll take my chances."

Stanley reached over to give a handshake and Fred reluctantly grasped the man's hand then quickly pulled away when he felt the cold, scaled skin.

On the way out Fred walked down a long corridor with an exit ahead. He glanced from side to side as he passed a series of doorways with windows. With mass production of cereal underway, one of the workers noticed as Fred watched through the glass and left the line to report the intruder. Quickly, he ran toward the exit and panicked when he saw Stanley and the guards headed in his direction.

With a severe tone Stanley bellowed "Oh, it is unfortunate that you have seen our top secret operation. We can't let you go now after seeing the manufacture of our special cereal. You should have cooperated when you had a chance. Now you will work here whether you like it or not. Guards, show our new worker to the employee quarters. Dinner is in one hour. Don't be late. We don't tolerate tardiness or impudence. Do as you are told and everything will be alright but if you do not cooperate fully, you will regret it."

Stanley held a device that would inject a tracking chip. Fred felt frightened and asked "What are they used for?"

Stanley replied "They serve as global tracking devices that are implanted in the human body. Eventually every person on the planet will have one of them. They store medical information, administer medication and manipulate behavior."

"The applications are infinite and extremely profitable. You will be given one as identification and once inserted it cannot be removed."

Out of the corner of his eye Fred noticed a worker appeared fatigued and in pain and when he massaged the insertion point of the chip, he became alert and content with a smile. Malevolent intent became immediately clear.

Guards led to another section and they forced Fred inside a small cubicle with only a bed, a chair and toilet. As he was shoved through the doorway, part of his shirt ripped, leaving fabric wedged in the lock.

He pushed his way out in to the hallway and headed to the nearest exit. An announcement over the speakers instructed all workers to assemble for dinner and when the crowd moved to the center of the complex, Fred continued to look for a way out.

Each exit led to another corridor, connected by conveyor belts and elevators. Chased and attacked by guards, watched on camera and captured, he was tied down on a medical table to receive the implant.

Kicking and screaming "Let me go, I refuse to let you violate my body. You won't get away with this."

Stanley removed a synthetic mask to reveal his true reptilian appearance and hissed "We have already gotten away with it and there is nothing you or anyone else can do about it. Our forces are poised at all of the pyramids for the final invasion of the human race."

In the hand of a technician, a large syringe was thrust in to Fred's arm and he screamed "NOOOOOOOOOO."

Bernard heard the scream and rushed in to Fred's room. He was in bed, kicking and screaming in fear, drenched with sweat.

He grabbed Fred's arm and shook it, then shouted "Wake up, Man. You are having a nightmare."

Relieved, Fred said "Oh thank God, the whole thing was a dream. You wouldn't believe what happened. Oh never mind the whole thing is ridiculous."

He got out of bed, took a shower and started the day. He had no appetite and felt disgusted with Bernard when he watched him consume a large stack of pancakes with butter and syrup with a glazed look in his eyes.

When Fred turned on the computer, Internet with all of the data saved had been deleted.

On television continuous commercials ran, advertising the high sugared products made by a subsidiary of ROT. People remained unaware of the invasion and continued consuming poison.

Although Fred felt overwhelmed by the enormous threat, he continued to do research at the library in an attempt to bring awareness to the situation and to expose the real truth. Everywhere he went he felt that he was being observed and believed that his behavior was being monitored. Soon, certain research material vanished from the shelves and his access to certain topics online became limited.

Messages from a secret entity began filling his email account with warnings that he had encroached on classified material. He was ordered to cease the research pertaining to the extraterrestrial presence on Earth. Two factions were apparently at play, Pleiadians and Draconians. Any research done on the subject was considered forbidden but Fred continued to dig for the truth.

Refusing to comply, Fred discovered that Pleiadians represented beings of light and wisdom and came to enlighten humans whereas Draconians emulated violence and came to Earth to destroy humanity.

One morning Bernard expected to see Fred at breakfast but he had vanished without a trace. All records of his existence had been deleted.

∞

When Al finished the story, Nate said "Wow that is a cool story but the part about reptilian invaders sounds too far-fetched. That research guy was too curious and got himself in to trouble. My dad says we should accept things and not make waves."

"The point of the story was to show that we are all being watched, studied, manipulated and controlled by media. At least you can realize the danger of sugar. Fred tried to reveal the truth but he was silenced."

Nate added "I dress how I want to dress and I eat what I want also. There is nothing wrong with sugar as long as you don't overdo it. As far as being controlled by media or aliens, that's ridiculous."

Al replied "Regardless of whether or not you believe in extraterrestrial intervention, sugar is a deadly poison and it is killing people but it tastes so good that it fools us in to thinking we are rewarding ourselves. I will tell you another story that illustrates my point."

Sweet Dreams

Halloween is a time of sweet delight for millions of children every year. They fill their stomachs with rich, delicious treats and quite often overindulge. After masquerading as pirates, zombies, monsters, vampires, witches and a variety of other characters the children gorge themselves on their "booty" of candy. For hyperactive children the sugar acts as a drug or stimulant and causes restless sleep and disturbing dreams.

Students of Hillcrest Middle School were preparing for the evening of trick or treat. Thirteen year olds, Damian and his twin brother Zack, dressed as a werewolf and vampire. Popular books and movie series influenced them and with their vivid imaginations, actually believed vampires and werewolves were real.

They dressed in black, wore gothic makeup and hairstyles and Damian went as far as filing his incisor teeth into fangs. Zack behaved as a predatory wolf and often howled at the girls in the class.

Damian and Zack were in a Special Education class, for their attention deficit and hyperactive disorder. Both of them had been moved from multiple foster homes and acted out aggressions to get attention.

None of the foster parents were able to connect with the boys and the disturbed teens retreated in to their own fantasy world. School was boring to them and they attempted to create trouble, just so they could be suspended. They played pranks on the teachers and other students and often got caught smoking in the bathroom. Neither of them cared what happened to them and both of them were on the verge of being expelled.

After being exiled from numerous foster homes they were currently being cared for by a childless couple Richard and Debra Martin. Although they treated the boys with love and respect, Damian and Zack didn't appreciate their kindness and continued to behave badly.

Posters of Wolfman and Dracula, Vlad the Impaler, decorated the walls of their room. Damian memorized Bram Stoker's Dracula and emulated the main character, a misunderstood, blood-sucking, vampire. They both watched films from the genre, over and over again.

Damian wore an Egyptian ankh pendant that represented eternal life around his neck and Zack wore a pentagram to ward off enemies. As the time went by, their behavior continually became more bizarre and frightening. Damian began using red food coloring in his water and pretended that he was drinking blood. Zack requested his meals included rare meat. Both boys continued to be belligerent toward authority.

Richard and Debra wanted to help them, but they felt powerless. The administration of the school warned that if the boys continued to misbehave, they would be expelled and sent to a juvenile detention facility.

At Halloween, Damian and Zack, donned their vampire and werewolf costumes and set out to terrorize the little kids and to steal their candy. By the end of the evening they were quite pleased with themselves and the mountains of candy. Chocolate, caramel, lollipops and other sweet delights were piled high on their beds.

Richard and Debra told them not to eat too much but they ignored them and each devoured several pounds of candy. Even though they both had terrible stomach aches, they continued to overindulge. Zack finally stopped when he felt sick. Damian drank a liter of red soda to wash down the confection and vomited.

Before they went to sleep, Richard came in to say good night and explained what the school councilor said about their behavior.

Richard said "I understand that you think behaving like a vampire and a werewolf is cool but it is a phase and hopefully you will outgrow it. Damian, I made a dentist appointment for you to fix your fangs. Zack, if we serve meat in this house, it is a privilege and will be prepared well done. It is time you two face reality."

Richard paused and stared at the boys then continued "Debra and I are willing to let you stay but you must obey our rules. I want you to think about what I have said and try to understand our point of view."

When Richard left the room Zack raised his middle finger to the door as Damian hissed and barred his fangs. Zack's stomach growled and he moaned in pain but he eventually fell asleep. Damian resented being told what to do and felt determined to keep his fangs. He pouted and whimpered until he also fell into a deep slumber.

Zack tossed and turned, lost in a nightmare. In the dream he was at a carnival with his girlfriend Tammy. They walked past a fortune teller's tent and were summoned inside by an old woman that pointed one of her fingers at them.

The Gypsy woman made a sign of warning and instructed them to sit for a tarot card reading. The light of the full moon illuminated the tent and cast strange shadows on the deck of cards. The first three cards of - Past, Present and Future were Death, Despair and Destruction.

The strange woman looked frightened and gave Zack a pentagram necklace and Tammy, a charm to protect her against evil. She made the sign of warning again and sent them away. The couple enjoyed the rest of the carnival and walked to Tammy's house.

The moon had risen high in the sky and illuminated the scene. Zack kissed Tammy, said good night and turned to leave as she went inside.

His skin began to burn and itch. Every fiber of his body felt searing pain and his head felt like it was exploding. Thick fur formed, starting with his head and moved down to his legs. Razor sharp claws protruded from his hands and feet and his muscles increased to triple the normal size. Zack's mouth jutted out and had rows of needle sharp teeth and a long, drooling tongue. The creature howled at the moon and roared with a mighty cry into the night.

Tammy removed her necklace and prepared to go to bed when she heard the blood-curdling roar. She looked outside and witnessed Zack's horrifying transformation. Zack burst through the door and attacked Tammy as she screamed for help.

Neighbors heard the commotion and surrounded the house. One of the men had a shotgun and fired at the wolf. Wounded, Zack was captured and taken to jail where he was tortured. Just as he was about to be branded with a hot iron, he woke up screaming in a pool of sweat. He realized that it was only a dream but it frightened him beyond reason. After that he swore never to pretend to be a werewolf, ever again.

Damian had a vivid dream that he was Vladimir the Impaler. In the 15th century Vlad III, Prince of Wallachia, was known as Dracula, Son of a Dragon. In Romanian, Dracul means Devil. Vlad and his brother were well-educated in combat, mathematics and science and they spoke several languages. It was a time of violence, bloodshed and plague.

From research Damian knew that Vlad had been was separated from his father and brother and was held in a prison cell. He was tortured, whipped and beaten for his stubborn attitude and his verbal abuse of others.

Despite the torture Vlad was defiant and refused to submit to his captors. He eventually was freed and he claimed his royal title. When he returned, he was horrified when he heard that his brother and father had been killed by the Ottomans. He became the Prince and ruled with a cruel hand.

All of Vlad's enemies were brutally slain. The impaled corpses were placed in a circular pattern around the intended enemy encampment and under Vlad's orders, entire towns were burned to the ground and all the people were killed.

While in captivity Vlad became obsessed with death and believed that if he ate the hearts of his victims, he would become more powerful. He began drinking fresh blood instead of wine and became addicted to the sensation of the warm liquid flowing down his throat.

Intoxicated with blood and power, Vlad continued to kill millions. He took great pleasure in tormenting others. The sadistic Prince spent his last days, penniless and demented. He was locked in a prison for the insane and forced to undergo painful treatments.

His body was pierced, poked and prodded and his abnormal behavior was studied. Vlad bit the ear off of one of the guards and escaped. He was captured and impaled, left to die a slow and excruciating death. Through the eyes of Vlad he saw the scene and experienced the pain, in vivid, gruesome detail.

Damian felt the sensation of warm blood dripping from his mouth when he bit the guard's ear. He grabbed the guard's sword, cut out his heart and took a bite while it was still beating. He also felt every agonizing moment of being impaled, hung on the spear for what seemed like weeks. After a long, agonizing experience, it was a great relief when he woke up from the horrible nightmare.

First thing in the morning Zack and Damian told each other about their terrifying dreams. When they realized that the large amount of sugar had caused the problem, they threw their candy in the garbage and cleared their room of all the occult paraphernalia, posters, books and movies.

Richard and Debra were both shocked when the boys came out for breakfast, dressed in regular clothes with no makeup. Damian agreed to go to the dentist to fix his teeth. Zack asked for his meat, well done. They returned to school and were on their best behavior.

From that moment on, both boys refused to eat candy and all sugared products. Ironically and miraculously they both recovered from their chronic health disorders. Richard and Debra adopted them and they never spoke of vampires or werewolves again.

∞

Al winked at Nate and said "I wouldn't drink so much of that red soda, you might be mistaken for a vampire."

"Ha, ha, dude, that's not funny. I love vampires and I'm not giving up my soda and candy. What about alcohol? Plenty of adults are alcoholics and they use booze to reward themselves. My parents drink all of the time and they are fine."

Shaking his head, Al said "They may seem fine but alcohol is even worse than sugar, for a variety of reasons. This tale is called Sails Unfurled- a term used to describe someone that has become demented and unhinged as a result of drinking alcohol."

Sails Unfurled

Sixty-five year old Jack Morgan lived in his own fantasy world of pirates where he experienced exciting adventures. He called himself Captain Jacques Morgan and believed that he was the fiercest pirate in history. No one, beside his wife Edna, understood that he was a gentle soul and would never intentionally harm himself or anyone else.

Jack carried a flask of spiced rum wherever he went. The flask was an antique from Barbados, purchased in a small shop while on vacation. The shopkeeper claimed the flask once belonged to a real pirate in Barbados. It inspired Jack's passion for pirates and he began to take on the personality of a wild buccaneer from the 17th century. He demanded to be called Captain or Sir at all times.

He loudly whistled or sang constantly and it became annoying to Edna.

The most repeated verses, "Fifteen men on a dead man's chest. Yo ho ho and a bottle of rum" and "What do you do with a drunken sailor, earlye in the morning."

He called Edna his Wench and demanded she wear skimpy revealing costumes. Her unconditional service and loyalty was absolutely required.

He constantly threatened to make her "walk the plank" or be "clapped in irons" if she didn't obey his every order.

Jack had been admitted to the hospital numerous times after consuming large amounts of rum and was suspected of attempting to commit suicide on several occasions. More than once he insisted that his ship-mates forced him to drink the rum or he would have been keel-hauled.

He swore that the flask kept refilling itself and he was obligated by pirate law to drink every drop of the so-called Sacred Elixir of the Gods. When released, he always continued the bizarre behavior.

He made the upper patio of their home in Florida into the deck of a pirate ship and watched the horizon daily, waiting for his "Mateys" to come and rescue him from his dreary life.

Jack shouted out commands and drove Edna close to madness. He spoke in nautical terms and insisted that his fellow pirates were waiting in bay to take him away to his private treasure cove in the Bermuda Triangle.

He continually watched the horizon through a spyglass or binoculars and steered his imaginary helm- an authentic steering wheel that was perched on the Crow's Nest- Jack's private fortress of solitude. If Edna dared to enter his domain, without his permission, he threatened bodily harm.

Once, after consuming rum for most of the day, while he was asleep, Edna went to the deck to clean up and collect laundry.

She accidently knocked over the steering wheel and woke up her husband. When he caught her in his private domain he became angry and vented his wrath toward Edna. He began to drink heavily from the flask, waved around a sharp sword and threatened his wife. She was accustomed to the verbal abuse but Jack's behavior was becoming frightening and intolerable.

He yelled "Bring me more rum, Wench. I'm only three sheets to the wind, not yet four."

Edna stared in amazement as the flask continued to fill itself as Jack continued to drink. She called the paramedics when he slipped and hit his head on the steering wheel. She loved Jack dearly, despite his eccentricities, and sought the help of Dr. Joel Benson, a well known Psychiatrist. Because of signs and severe symptoms of alcoholism, the doctor advised Edna to admit Jack to the Seaside Sanitarium for observation.

Dr. Benson was famous for his treatments using hypnosis and past-life regression. Edna believed Dr. Benson and the Seaside facility would be able to treat her husband for his addiction and cure his deluded mental condition.

The sanitarium overlooked the ocean and Edna thought the crisp salty air and professional care would bring her husband back to reality. She wished for him to come back home, sane and sober.

At the hospital, the next day, Jack woke up with the worst headache and hangover of his entire life. He was angry with Edna for admitting him to the "Looney Bin" and began verbally abusing the hospital staff. He hurled insults at the nurses, using pirate phrases, and tossed his food around his room and called it Bilge Slop. He demanded to be released and became increasingly agitated when ignored. One night Jack left his bed and entered the patient common area.

Some of the patients became upset when Jack jumped up on the table and shouted "Alas me hearties, it is I, Captain Morgan. Seize the day and rebel against your captors. Escape with me and I'll take ye away from this prison. Ahoy mateys, the Papillion is on its way!"

Jack swaggered around the room and began singing. Several of the male patients joined him in a chorus of "Yo, Ho, Ho and a bottle of rum."

The patients started to enjoy the moment until Dr. Benson stopped them. The staff administered sedatives to all and locked Jack in his private room.

Being in captivity drove him further into his dementia. Given large amounts of sedatives, he retreated into another existence where he had no total control of his surroundings.

Dr. Benson planned to study Jack's reaction to hypnosis, while an experimental drug was used to put the patient in an altered state, where they revealed their innermost thoughts and desires. He believed Jack's condition was acute alcoholism but was fascinated by his unusual behavior. Other patients with similar conditions were cured by hypnosis and Dr. Benson believed that Jack could be cured as well.

The doctor decided to try a new untested technique on Jack, in the attempt to completely diagnose the situation. He felt it was worth the risk to find a cure for Jack's illness and although she was hesitant, he convinced Edna to sign the proper documents.

The drug was administered and electronic devices placed on Jack's skull, linked directly to a computer interface. Images and thought-waves were then received by the monitor and placed the mind of the doctor.

A headset worn by the physician controlled the treatment and was programmed to shut down when danger was eminent. If not used properly, the technique could cause permanent brain damage to the patient and the doctor.

The doctor checked the timer on the failsafe switch and began to countdown from 100. It only took a few moments for Jack to connect to the interface. Dr. Benson placed the headset device over his temples and entered Jack's private domain. Although the images were in virtual reality, the sensations seemed vividly realistic.

In the alternate world, the doctor existed as Joel DuBois, an untrustworthy, ambitious pirate. The ship was called the Papillion, French for butterfly and known as the fastest and most heavily armed galleon of all the pirate ships in the Bermuda and Caribbean Islands. It appeared to be a silver saucer with butterfly wings for sails.

The session continued-Joel pleaded with Jack to share the secret. "Captain, have I not served you well? Why will you not say where our treasure is located? I have a right to know. I am your loyal friend!"

The captain paused then growled "You will never know my secret. You are a traitor! You think I do not know of your treacherous plot to keep me intoxicated so you can murder me and assume command of the Papillion. I am aware of everything on my ship."

Joel screamed "You may be the Captain of the Papillion, but I am the Admiral of the Saucer Fleet! They are on their way to kill you and take your ship!"

Jack replied "There is no brigade coming to save you. Ye are a bloody, daft fool and the secret of our treasure is not safe with the likes of ye."

The two men struggled over the wheel and tumbled into a fight on the bridge. The Papillion lost wind power, fell into the ocean and they crashed in the water, near Florida. The men continued to argue about the treasure. Jack refused to share any information with Joel and the fight escalated. Joel picked up a heavy rock and threw it at Jack's face. In a rage, they began to strangle each other.

The failsafe device sensed the danger and the two men were awakened from the hypnotic trance. Jack awakened completely free of his delusions. He was happy, peaceful and sober for the first time in months.

Being a pirate became a vague memory from a wild, alcohol induced, dream but after he achieved his sobriety, he kept his interest in ships, flying saucers and treasure maps. When Jack was released and returned home Edna greeted him with open arms.

She had disposed of all alcohol and the antique flask. The steering wheel was covered with a tarp and all signs of pirates removed from the house. When he returned to the Crow's Nest, instead of his odd demeanor, Jack silently watched the ocean from the patio and meditated.

As a result of the hypnosis, the doctor also gained an affinity for pirates. Grateful for having her husband back, as a gift of appreciation, Edna gave the antique flask to Dr. Benson to add to his collection of nautical objects.

Pleased by the gift, Joel was overcome by the urge to pick up the flask and examined it. The tarnished silver, engraved with the letters Le Papillion, depicted a design of a ship with butterfly wings.

Later, Dr. Benson used to headset to record his observations of Jack Morgan's case. While studying the data, his mind was dominated and taken over by the spirit of the pirate Joel Benson Dubois. He raised the flask of rum to his lips and drank heavily as the flask refilled itself again and again.

When completely intoxicated the doctor grabbed a cane and began waving it like a sword. He shouted "Alas me hearties. Come away with me or walk the plank. Ship ahoy. Full speed ahead-sails unfurled."

The orderlies restrained the doctor and attempted to put him in a straight jacket but he struggled and broke away. He kept shouting, ran outside to the edge of the cliff and threw himself over the edge, while the staff helplessly watched.

At the same time, from the roof, Jack was watching the horizon with his spyglass and saw a most incredible sight. An enormous silver flying saucer descended, entered the harbor and rescued a man from drowning in the tide.

The ship was then greeted by a brigade of other saucer ships. Jack's jaw dropped and his eyes bulged when the giant wings opened, dragonfly oars appeared out of portholes and the fantastic ship lifted the man out of the water.

After Dr. Benson's tragic, apparent death, the untested device was ultimately blamed for his accidental suicide, even though his body was never found.

Jack Morgan never drank another drop of alcohol but continued to see flying saucers coming and going from the surface. He and Edna bought a sailboat and called it Le Petit Papillion, the Little Butterfly. One of Jack's maps had the coordinates to an island in center of the Bermuda Triangle, marked with the crest of Le Papillion. They headed out on an adventure to find buried treasure but were never seen again.

∞

At the conclusion of the story, Al said "Actually Jack and Edna were taken aboard a saucer craft by inter-dimensional extraterrestrials. Are you beginning to understand that what I say is true?"

Nate said "Well maybe I agree that alcohol and sugar are bad news but it is too hard to believe that some drunk dude that thinks he is a pirate and his wife got abducted by aliens."

Nate added " I seriously doubt that we are being watched and monitored by some secret society and I definitely don't believe in flying saucers."

With a sigh, Al replied "This may shed light on that subject. Pay close attention and try to understand the meaning. This is a good example of how secret societies have controlled the world for centuries. There is a saying- Truth will set you free, but sometimes truth comes at a high price."

Fountain of Dreams

Brooke Mason despised her job as a bank teller and desperately wished to pursue a career as a news photographer. She had a keen eye for design and chose unique subjects. While walking to work every day she passed a water fountain in the center of a beautiful park and always tossed her coins into the fountain to make wishes.

The Fountain of Dreams was built in 1780 by Brooke's ancestor, Nathaniel Edward Mason. Allegedly the Mason family was part of an elite secret society that controlled the economy and provided service to the public. She became curious about the society and began research.

The fountain's base, inscribed with the words "The Truth Shall Set You Free" was built to honor the founding fathers of America. Coins from all of the many local fountains were gathered and used to fund various humanitarian projects. Allegedly the money was used to build hospitals, schools and banks and helped to feed needy families.

After work she studied in stacks of books attempting to find information about secret societies. She found out that a malevolent brotherhood, that involved a dark plan of dominance in world banking, existed and had ties to the bank where she worked.

Thousands of dollars passed through her hands everyday and she carefully recorded the transactions. She noticed that U.S. currency illustrates many of the symbols used by modern society. The eye, inside the capstone of a pyramid, has various meanings.

Brooke learned that it was the "all-seeing eye of knowledge" and symbolized enlightenment. She discovered it also had meaning in Ancient Egypt and was the symbol for wisdom, wealth and prosperity, known as the Eye of Horus. It was a symbol used by US Treasury, Knights Templar, Freemasons and represented New World Order. On the US Dollar, the symbol means eye of providence, strength and duration. She also learned that the thirteen steps of the pyramid represented the original thirteen states. The phrase above the eye Annuit Coeptis, means "He has favored our undertakings."

Novus Ordo Seclorum signifies "New Order of the ages and birth of the United States of America. The slogan on much of the US currency is printed with "E Plurbus Unum- Of many-one, stands for the union of states in one united government. .

Most of the articles presented views pertaining to a vast network, set in place by an elite and wealthy group of powerful people. The network allegedly infiltrated every aspect of world economy and government and according to the information, the elite few dominate and controlled the masses. It was compared to puppet-masters, in control of the strings. The symbol of the all-seeing eye represented absolute power and control of all economic resources.

She was able to trace her family tree back to the 1780's and desired to learn more. The story of Nathaniel Mason was a mystery that Brooke was determined to solve. Confused by the conflicting ideas, Brooke took her camera and went to the Fountain of Dreams, to think. The historical plaza around the fountain was quiet and made her feel peaceful.

The bank where she worked had been built around the same time as the fountain and was near the park. Brooke meditated with her head full of questions. Sunset illuminated the outside of the bank and fountain which caught her photographic eye. As she snapped a few pictures, Brooke noticed that a group of businessmen in black suits, wearing sunglasses entered through the rear of the bank. Above the doorway was the all-seeing eye within the shape of a pyramid. Someone in the shadows observed her as she continued to take pictures.

Before going to bed, she sent the pictures to her friend Ben Nelson, a reporter for an alternative news network.

The next day she went to work as usual and went to count the money in her drawer. Her cash drawer was empty and she entered the supervisor's office. He loudly spoke with someone on the phone and then slammed down the receiver. The unpleasant supervisor of the bank was from a wealthy family who owned and operated the branch.

Brooke said "Sorry to disturb you, Mr. Hallstead, my cash drawer is empty. What would you like me to do?"

In a rough voice he replied "Don't bother me right now. Go to the vault and get a fresh drawer and we will discuss it later!"

Before leaving the office, Brooke noticed numerous strips, used to wrap 100 dollar bills, had been tossed in the garbage can. She noticed Hallstead was glaring at her and left quickly.

A corridor led down a steep staircase to an elevator shaft and with a special code, the tellers were allowed access to the vault for a brief time and were photographed the entire time. Brooke collected the cash drawer and when it was pulled it out of the slot, she noticed the symbol of the all-seeing eye on the wall behind it.

Suddenly the vault door slammed shut and locked. Emergency lights came on and Brooke panicked. Another door opened and revealed a secret corridor.

She followed the sounds of chanting and arrived in the midst of a ceremony with shrouded figures that danced around a fountain shrine. Men with dark masks entered the chamber and circled around Brooke. A strong arm grabbed her and forced her to lie on the altar.

A shrouded figure approached and when he removed the hood, it revealed the face of Jason A. Hallstead, Bank Manager.

"Miss Mason, it is unfortunate that you have stumbled upon our sanctuary but you won't live long enough to tell anyone."

"What are you talking about? I don't know anything about your business. I'm just a teller and an amateur photographer."

With condescending tone Hallstead grumbled "Yes that is why you are here. We noticed you taking pictures at the fountain and you caught some of us arriving for the ritual. We cannot afford for anyone to recognize us. We are of an elite society and have been using the money derived from the coins in the fountain, although it is a small pittance, for decades."

Brooke snapped "What gives you the right to take away the dreams of others?"

"We represent the wealthy and elite and the public will never know the truth."

Ben received the pictures from Brooke and recognized several of the men. He reported them as wanted felons that had been responsible for acts of terrorism and had also been under investigation for fraud, embezzling and cyber-espionage.

When Brooke failed to return to her station, her fellow employees noticed but in fear of Mr. Hallstead, said nothing. When Ben arrived at the bank, accompanied by federal agents, they were denied entry and not allowed to ask questions. Used to getting his own way, Ben proceeded to wander in the corridors behind the bank and looked for Brooke. When he could not find her, he went outside and waited by the fountain with the agents.

With Brooke as prisoner, Hallstead returned to his office and when he left for the day, he walked to the fountain and Ben watched him as he entered through a door.

Ben instructed the agents to remain outside while he followed Hallstead. When he entered the corridor and heard chanting, he arrived at the scene of a strange ritual. He saw Brooke tied up to a post with a gag over her mouth.

While Hallstead and the others discussed the situation, Ben crawled over and released Brooke. They attempted to escape but before they could get away, Hallstead noticed and they both were taken into custody.

With plans to execute the intruders, Hallstead prepared his instruments of torture. With a searing hot knife in his hand, Hallstead raised his arm and poised himself to stab Ben. Fortunately the federal agents found them in time, just as Hallstead was about to kill them both. The group of criminals were taken into custody and charged with treason, espionage and theft.

Photographs of the fountain and the exposure of the criminals launched Brooke's new career as a reporter and she worked closely with the police. Her fondest wish came true but in fear, she never again spoke of the experience or divulged information about secret societies to anyone.

Truth ultimately set her free but she remained under constant surveillance by an anonymous secret society. Her friend Ben Nelson disappeared and was never seen again."

∞

Al said "Now do you get what I mean about secret societies? If you speak out and try to expose them, you get silenced, one way or another."

Nate sneered "I suppose so but there is no way I will believe in secret organizations that control banking and I refuse to acknowledge that extraterrestrial visitors are among us."

Al said "Okay, well this is a good story and even though it is about the future, it will happen."

Nate snapped "How do you know?"

With a grin, Al replied "I know because I was there. This next story is absolutely true but you won't believe it. It will explain everything I have told you but you must open your mind and go beyond the limits of your beliefs. Listen carefully."

Maiden Voyage

A large crowd attended the opening of the infamous Area 51, believed to have housed a secret research facility for over a century. Media representatives flocked to the site, expecting to see an underground laboratory and alien space-craft. For many decades, unidentified flying objects and strange phenomenon were associated with the desolate area and as a result, people who believed Earth was being visited by extraterrestrials gathered together for the event.

Despite all the stories and theories the grounds were void of any evidence of recent use and the old buildings were all falling apart. The crowd gathered near an airplane hangar, around a platform with a podium, set-up for a presentation.

A tall, thin man approached the microphone, cleared his throat and said "Ladies and Gentlemen, you are all here to witness the unveiling of the truth. For many decades this land around Area 51 has been subject to criticism, speculation and dispute. We have opened the inner chambers below the desert to the public, to prove that there are no, or have there ever been, aliens or space ships here. Feel free to explore the grounds and lower levels."

A man shouted "Aliens are here! They live in the Antarctic have been here for centuries observing us!"

"That is absurd. There are no such things as aliens from space."

"What about all the UFO sightings and abductions? I was taken and I know a lot of people who also have been."

Others began to tell their stories of abduction and alien encounters. Heated arguments broke-out between believers and those who had a logical explanation for all the events.

The announcer said "Everyone, please listen. All of those sightings resulted from mass mind control by the media. No one has ever proved the existence of beings from another world and the only images we have are manufactured by the entertainment industry. Human technology has provided the advances in space exploration, not technology from outer space!"

After a few questions from the crowd, the announcer continued "The work done here was strictly for defensive purposes. In the event of invasion from other countries or natural phenomenon, such as asteroids or solar flares, strategic steps needed to be taken."

"Why have there been so many reports of UFOs?"

"The only space-craft were ones designed by our own military and it was essential to keep the information classified, top secret."

Curious onlookers searched the grounds for clues. Prior to the event the former contents of Area 51 had been moved to the new location, a station on the moon. Small crafts, designed to look like flying saucers, transported equipment and supplies to the base. The secret move had been gradual and during the process, any report of a UFO excused as a hoax.

The secret observatory and research lab on the Moon had been developed by a group of rogue scientists and mercenaries, called ORION- Organization of Revolution and Insurrection of Nations. Their plan involved achieving absolute power and world domination. The group had accumulated vast wealth for decades and planned their strategic moves carefully from a base in the Antarctic.

The leader of the militant group was a diabolical, narcissistic, obsessed with power. Dr. Sebastian Evans and his followers staged an elaborate hoax, in an effort to control the minds of the population of Earth. Their sole purpose was to cause civil unrest and to control the masses with their own propaganda. They wanted to create a New World Order with ORION as the supreme controlling power.

Deep below the surface of the Moon, Area 51 had been carefully reconstructed. Masquerading as aliens from another planet, experiments were performed on subjects abducted from various locations on Earth. Dozens of human beings were studied and used in the horrifying experiments. Mind control, chemical and biological weapons and mind altering drugs were used on the helpless victims.

Many living beings suffered brutal treatment and if the subjects survived the experiments, their memories were erased. On a few occasions abductees were returned to their homes to tell their stories but they were treated as mental patients.

The events were carefully orchestrated to appear as an alien invasion and the plan to cause widespread fear and panic had been very successful. Part of the mind control was making people believe in an alien threat, in order to divert from the real threat from fellow humans.

After touring Area 51 and being disappointed, the reporters left the area to cover another story. The next media event was the launch of the first solar powered, airship-the SS Stratos, a cruise-liner capable of orbiting Earth and docking on the Moon.

After visiting Area 51 and interviewing people that claimed to have been abducted by extraterrestrials, reporter Bill Carson booked passage on the SS Stratos. From what he had gathered, he believed that something sinister was happening on the Moon and planned to investigate.

Highly skilled Doctors, Astronauts, Navigators and Technicians along with the most elite and wealthy patrons were allowed on the voyage. Passengers were selected and exclusively invited to participate, based on their financial status, power and influence.

Shuttle pilots flew their small aircraft back and forth to the SS Stratos. Luggage and supplies were loaded ahead of the passengers. Bill and a crew of twelve from the Global Media Network were chosen to cover the story of the launch and maiden voyage. They interviewed passengers while they waited to board.

The ship launched on schedule and when it lifted slowly off the ground, it rotated several times. Rockets, blasted from the lower levels, thrust it into the atmosphere.

When the news crew entered the dining area, a herald of trumpets announced the arrival of the royalty, ambassadors, bank owners, oil moguls and a variety of celebrities as they paraded in front of the cameras.

The display impressed Bill and the others as champagne flowed from fountains made of gold and ice sculptures decorated the tables of tantalizing food. Exotic foods from all over the world and the finest liquor was brought onboard and generously served to all guests. With unlimited food, alcohol, gambling or entertainment, every wish was gladly fulfilled by the attentive crew members.

Extravagant shows and a wide variety of activities created a pleasant environment for the passengers. Workers on the SS Stratos provided excellent services and the owners depended on the staff to bring in funding for the new colony on the Moon.

At dinner, the Captain announced "Ladies and Gentlemen, we are at maximum orbit now, so please enjoy the view of our fabulous planet. You should be able to see the African continent and the vast deserts. Note the Great Pyramids of Giza are distinct, even from this distance. We will complete one full orbit and then we'll dock at Lunar Port 1. You will be the very first civilians to see the amazing feat of architecture and modern technology in person. Enjoy the voyage!"

Bill slipped away from the dining room to explore on his own. Long corridors led to rows of doors, rooms and elevators. He noticed bright orange radiation signs warning him to stay away from the lower level of the ship. A ladder led to an open hatch and he heard voices from below.

"Hurry up and put those weapons away. We can't afford for anyone to find out what's going on."

"I know, you don't have to yell at me. Keep your voice down. Those idiotic passengers won't find out, they are too busy indulging themselves."

"Did the drugs get added the food yet? I want to be sure that the chocolate and champagne fountains provide a constant supply of tranquilizers."

"Yes, I put the bags of sugar, laced with the substance provided, in the pantry. They won't suspect a thing- they will be intoxicated and oblivious."

Bill felt stunned and when the men left, he felt compelled to investigate further. He climbed down a ladder to a storage area that was filled with crates marked ORION. Someone came from behind, struck him on the head and he fell on the floor, unconscious.

After circling the globe, the navigator set the coordinates and locked trajectory to the Moon. Several days later the ship arrived, a platform appeared on the lunar surface and a series of lights led to a smooth landing. By the time they arrived, the passengers were completely intoxicated, lethargic and oblivious to any danger.

Bill's head throbbed and with blurred vision he studied his surroundings. He was alone, strapped on a table in an examination room and heard voices from behind a partition.

With gruff voice, a man said "Let me see the device! I've waited long enough for my prize. It had better be worth the credits I paid!"

Another man said "It is definitely worth more than credits. With this device you will be able to control the minds of everyone on the planet. We found it inside a space-ship that crashed near Area 51 a long time ago. The entire complex in the desert has been dismantled and transferred to Lunar Port 1. We have discovered that the device is from a race of beings called Pleiadians. They have been visiting Earth for centuries and have been trying to communicate with us."

"An alien's body was found in the wreckage and when it was thoroughly examined, they found that it was a robot. It seemed to be powered by a this device and has an unknown energy source. Scientists studied the object and discovered that it served as a probe with the ability to communicate with humans on a subliminal level. They also found out that it could control minds."

" Good, that is what I wanted to hear. We have waited a long time to make our move. No one will dare challenge us once they believe we saved them from a malevolent alien invasion."

"Yes, we will prevail. There are thousands of saucer-crafts ready that we have built and we have prepared the masses by planting seeds of discontent. We will fool them in to believing Earth is under attack by hostile aliens forces and then come to the rescue. It's a brilliant plan. Get the saucers ready and tell the ORION Squadron to prepare for attack!"

"Yes, Dr. Evans." Panic-stricken after hearing the plot, Bill struggled to break free of his bonds. He was familiar with the notorious ORION and realized the eminent danger. He managed to loosen the straps and escaped while the conversation continued. When he returned to the dining room to find the others, he saw that all of the passengers had been drugged and he was the only one that was still awake and alert.

While the passengers continued to eat, drink and sleep, hundreds of saucer-crafts emerged from hangar at Lunar Port 1. Ships prepared to launch and as the people began to wake up, they observed the massive fleet hovering outside the ship.

ORION members disguised themselves as Draconians, reptilian invaders, and presented a terrifying display of power. Laser weapons, sirens and flashing lights gave the impression of malevolent force.

All of the people were summoned and gathered in the dining room. The apparent leader of the invasion stood in front of the crowd and held a glowing sphere of blue light in his hands. A sound was emitted from the sphere that caused everyone to cover their ears. The passengers were terrified as they were surrounded by a hoard of armed reptilian creatures.

Just as planned, Dr. Evans had control of the situation. He and his battalion appeared to arrive just in time to save the passengers. The staged production fooled everyone into believing ORION had been the saving grace.

Saucers were destroyed for everyone to witness and after a mock battle, the creatures appeared to be killed. The crowd cheered when it appeared as though the "Aliens" had been defeated.

News of the attack caused wide-spread panic on Earth. People scrambled and poised to defend themselves against invaders. Earth went on high-alert and Dr. Evans took advantage of the situation.

Bill stayed hidden and filmed the entire incident. From his locked room, he broadcasted the report that the passengers of SS Stratos had become hostages of Dr. Sebastian Evans and they all were victims of a hoax. After the first broadcast he vanished along with his camera.

In an attempt to use the device on passengers, Dr. Evans unknowingly sent a distress call to the Pleiadians. He convinced the others to acknowledge ORION as the new world government and to declare himself as supreme ruler.

On Pleiades, the signal was received by the Supreme Council of Planets. News of the event at Lunar Port 1, reached the fleet and within a short time, ships headed to Earth. As in the past, emissaries went to Earth at pivotal moments in history to observe the human race.

Pleiadians, highly intelligent and peaceful beings, had been searching for a new home because the sun was burning out and they were doomed unless they could find a compatible planet to relocate their civilization. A fleet of space ships stayed ready to defend against their enemies, Draconians, and remained concealed behind the tail of a comet.

Although they abhorred violence and confrontation, the Pleiadian Fleet was sent to Earth to intervene. They had no weapons of any kind and the key to power was in their defensive shield, generated by a collective mind. All minds merged into one peaceful entity and appeared as a fleet of silver orbs.

ORION made its headquarters in the Antarctic and assembled nuclear weapons to be used as leverage. When the fleet appeared, Supreme Chancellor Evans and called upon all military forces and declared war on the alien invaders.

Out of ignorance and fear, all countries of Earth opened the arsenal of weapons and attacked the Pleiadian Fleet. However, the attack had no impact on the aliens.

The full force of weapons was reflected back on to Earth and as a result, all life was extinguished, leaving only the surface of the planet intact.

A signal sent by the fleet was received by the Supreme Council that read- We have found an uninhabited new home. Prepare for the Maiden Voyage to Earth.

∞

Nate clucked his tongue "That story is so stupid. There is no way you can convince me that we are being controlled by aliens. We would blow them out of the sky if they tried to take over. Besides, we are still here and even if they do come, humans will prevail."

Al looked up at the sky and said "They are already here and have been for centuries. Humans are only a small part of the overall picture and our egos are insignificant. I will tell you one more story and if this doesn't open your mind, I give up."

Silver Seed

Earth, 2099

A private corporation sponsored the first voyage to the nearest planet outside of Earth's solar system. Alpha Centauri Prime was considered to be the most likely to sustain humanoid life. The ship resembled a lotus flower in a closed position and when it was opened it appeared as an oval disc that resembled a silver seed.

The ship Silver Seed could transport five hundred people. Embryos of humans and animals were frozen in stasis to populate the new colony. Specimens of plants, flowers, seeds and trees from all parts of the world were carefully preserved and carried on the voyage.

With limited space a lottery was held to decide who would be included on the voyage and who would be left behind. Pollution of the environment had made the planet nearly uninhabitable. It was predicted that Earth would be void of life within the next century.

Dr. Edward Black designed the Silver Seed to use the Earth's gravity to hurl the ship beyond the reaches of the solar system. When they reached the boundary, the theory was to use the gravity of Alpha Centauri Prime to pull them the remainder of the way.

Dr. Alex Ross disagreed with Black's theory and believed that they would not reach the boundaries of the solar system, due to the radiation belt that surrounded Earth. Ross explained that if a space craft attempted to cross the belt, the Boomerang Effect would occur. He believed that Silver Seed would be pulled back to Earth when it had exceeded the force used to propel them. He also believed that if they were able to reach the edge of the solar system, Alpha Centauri Prime's gravitational field would not be strong enough to prevent the ship from the effect.

Dr. Black did not believe in the Boomerang Effect. He theorized that the solar system was linear and based mathematical calculations, plotted the course on a straight line to Alpha Centauri Prime. Dr. Ross insisted that the universe was elliptical and claimed that all objects and beings are subject to unknown forces of nature and if they leave the confines of the planet, they returned to their places of origin, in another time-dimension.

The men continued to dispute the issues but eventually the seniority of Dr. Black prevailed. Five hundred people were selected, representing every race and religion from the Earth and were to be placed in stasis for the long trip.

Calculations predicted it would take at least one hundred years to reach their destination. Children of the voyagers would return to Earth with news of a new home.

Millions of eager onlookers gathered at the site to witness the launch of Silver Seed. People joined in a prayer to bless the mission and many of them knew that if it failed, Earth and all inhabitants were doomed to extinction.

The launch went as planned and the passengers were in suspended animation with the exception of Black and Ross. They also were going to be in stasis eventually but they waited to make sure everything was going according to the plan.

Dr. Black's plan was to use the other planets in the solar system as propellers. The forces of gravity would then guide the Silver Seed along the correct path toward Alpha Centauri Prime.

Dr. Ross knew of the danger of the radiation belt and continually warned his associate that if they reached the edge of the solar system, the radiation would destroy all life and the craft would be propelled back to Earth by the Boomerang Effect. The doctors continued to disagree up until the time they both entered the stasis chambers. Dr. Ross pretended to sleep and when Dr. Black was deep in slumber, he chose to stay awake in order to observe.

The ship left the known boundaries and as it passed through the trail of a comet, it was bombarded with concentrated radiation. When the ship reached Saturn, it was captured by the gravitational pull of the gaseous rings. Silver Seed was hurled around the planet and shot back, just as Dr. Ross had predicted. It followed the same path as the comet and headed directly toward Earth.

On Earth, after the Silver Seed launched, people competed for any and all resources. Each country guarded their boundaries and amassed supplies. World panic spread when it was reported that a comet was headed for the Moon. With little time left, people fought one another and eventually orders were given to begin nuclear war. Within a short time, all human and animal life had been destroyed.

By the time Silver Seed returned to Earth, the entire population had vanished along with animals and all wildlife. The comet missed the moon by a short distance and briefly caused storms, earthquakes and tidal waves. History, time and Earth's geography changed as a result.

Onboard Silver Seed, at the correct time, passengers awakened and believed that they had reached Alpha Centauri Prime. Colonists were amazed by the similarities between Earth and their new home, including the existence of pyramids. They unloaded their supplies and began to build a new civilization.

Dr. Ross knew that they had been hurled thousands of years backward in time but remained silent. He prayed that humans would not make the same mistakes and would find a way to live in peace.

∞

At the conclusion of the session with Al, Nate laughed and announced "That is the most ridiculous bunch of crap that I have ever heard. Maybe you are just a crazy old hippie."

Al winked, smiled and replied "So you think, but everything I told you is true. The secret of time travel is based on the alignment of the pyramids. Given the correct frequencies, we are capable of foretelling the future as well as revisiting the past."

Sneering, Nate retorted "How do you know what is going to happen in the distant future? Are you psychic?"

After a brief pause, Al said "Not a psychic, a time traveler. I told you that I was there. My name is Dr. Alex Ross."

Nate scratched his head in confusion and walked away. When he turned around to say good bye, he saw Al walking down the beach. Intrigued and curious, he followed.

At sunset, oblong clouds gathered above, Nate stared in awe at the horizon when a large space craft, shaped as a silver seed, emerged.

Al raised his arms to signal and he was transported aboard. In an instant, the time-ship disappeared. Nate thought that he had imagined it and went home.

The next day Nate returned to the angel statue and asked the vendors about Al and was told that he was called Venice Beach Angel and was a vagabond that occasionally visited to tell stories to the tourists.

One of the merchants said "He is a harmless old hippie that took too much acid in the 60s. He claims to be a time traveler and supposedly rides around in a silver flying saucer. Isn't that a hoot?"

The experience compelled Nate to begin researching conspiracy theories, time travel and extraterrestrial visitors. A page concerning reptilian invaders caught his attention and it led to classified information concerning sugar used for mind-control of the masses and showed details of a plot to depopulate the planet.

Nate's father walked in the room and when he saw the symbol that represented the secret society, in which he was an active member, he sternly warned "Don't make waves Son and quit reading about this sort of thing, it is dangerous."

Soon after telling his father about his visit with Al and theories regarding space ships that traveled in time, Nate stopped the research and no one heard from him again.

3,000 BC

Imhotep, an architect, supervised the building of the first pyramid and discovered correlation between dimensions of the structure in alignment with certain constant stars. Using the brightest point to the north, used as a compass, he planned that all structures would be in perfect alignment.

At the same time that the pyramid was complete and in alignment to Pleiades in the Orion star system, a vortex opened up in the sky. A large saucer craft emerged and landed near the structure.

Thousands of people, including Nikola Tesla, Dr. Alex Ross, Fred Marino, Edna and Jack Morgan, Dr. Joel Benson, Ben Nelson, Bill Carson and Nate Miller, along with a multitude of animals and birds, disembarked.

When the ship opened the hatches and the passengers resembled the figures from their religion, Imhotep and the others dropped to their knees and welcomed the arrival of supernatural entities that they believed were Gods.

The End

©Kathleen Staley 2017

Made in the USA
Las Vegas, NV
02 December 2021